Silent Fortune

JANET CARAFA

DENVER, COLORADO

Contents

Introduction

The point of view of a Mime Artist

As a Mime Artist, I am amazed at people's reactions when I am performing mime. Many automatically stop speaking and start to express themselves physically. They may start to mouth words and wave their arms in order to communicate with the Mime. And many start dancing! In fact, I have seen an entire room of people, standing still and chatting, suddenly start dancing when the Mime enters the room! There are always strong reactions – and they always happen immediately – beyond immediately. It happens before I notice!

What is happening as we communicate without words? My guess is that when I am silently interacting, our intuition is allowed in the forefront instead of our analytical mind. I call it communication from the heart. Whatever you call it – it is the way human beings communicate in the larger sense. Words are learned and therefore are the *secondary* form of communication. *Intuition is first and foremost.*

One wonderful and enlightening experience I had was performing mime in the Museum of Transportation. It is a museum where you can climb on the trolley car and have hands-on experience of the different exhibits. Silently I mimed, travelling through the museum with a group of children. For an hour we silently played together and explored the museum having fun. When it was time to go home, one of the children, a 3 year old, silently motioned to me to come close so she could whisper in my ear. "How do you speak so softly?" she whispered. I had never spoken a word.

And so, as a Mime Artist, my point of view is that each one of us is 100% intuitive—first and foremost and beyond our five senses. We are born with this ability. We each see the invisible, hear silence and are creative beings—it is our essence. Here, amidst our noisy fast paced lives, each of us is innately and spontaneously creative and intuitive with invisible colors that glow around us as we express ourselves in an ever changing world! Enter here... go beyond your sound barrier and see for yourself!

Silent Fortune

Episode 1 —THE LION'S DREAM

Go beyond the sound barrier

ENTER HERE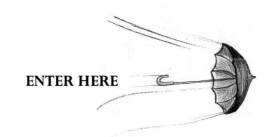

Chapter 1:
Silent Land in the Sky

U p above, it was a beautiful windy day in the clouds. The rays of the shining sun spread far and wide over the place known as Silent Land in the Sky. Silent Land is made of pristine clouds that glisten and move with the wind, floating high above the lands of planet Earth. People called Mimes live here in buildings made of clouds that constantly shift with the wind. Nothing stays the same in Silent Land in the Sky. Yes, change is constant for the Mimes of Silent Land, as nothing is solid or still. This ongoing ever changing flow creates a symphony of motion – it is like a silent song. It is never heard but, instead, it is felt. This is normal when you live in the clouds.

Mimes in Silent Land have never spoken words, heard sounds or made sounds – thus the name. They express themselves with body language and eye contact and communicate without words. And, when they express themselves, *colors* appear instead of sound! Different vivid colors flash, glow and flow from the movements and the thoughts of the Mimes creating magnificent radiant swirls of color. Every movement a Mime makes becomes a colorful, silent communication. Every thought and feeling a Mime has creates a colorful painting in the sky. Silent Land in the sky is truly an ever-changing work of art. And yes, this is normal here too.

Circling above and below Silent Land is a rainbow surrounding the land all around. It has always been here as far as all Mimes can remember – from before Mime Time Memory. The rainbow holds every color of the spectrum. And guess what—that is also normal here.

All is Silent.

There is absolutely no sound at all. And, of course, this is normal too.

On this strange and beautiful day, the sun's rays sparkled against the bright blue sky and gleamed on the rainbow circling Silent Land. The many colors of this cloud world swirled and glowed brightly, and the cloud buildings shifted even more than usual. As the cloud cuckoo clock on the town hall silently struck three, something wasn't quite right. The Mimes were picnicking just within the cloud-formed arch that marked the entrance to Silent Land. It seemed as if things were normal—in colorful silence. Nobody noticed that someone was missing, but Fortune the Mime was nowhere to be seen.

Fortune had created quite a stir that week by causing an incident that had shocked and confused the Mime community. Since the incident, she had spent a lot of time on her own. So, for the moment, things were back to normal and no one gave it much thought. In fact, on this day in Silent Land, there was an air of relief in the Mime community.

Children and adults, the community of mimes—hundreds of them—were there together. Some played ball, some did the afternoon cloud dance, some bounced high and some finished eating lunch– all seemed to be as usual, with colors glowing and flowing silently.

But the colors in the distance were shifting slowly and eerily. There was an unseen blue violet mist of sadness that was seeping along the horizon - a mist that spread slowly and drearily. But no one seemed to notice. The mimes played and frolicked together in swirling rainbows of the most vibrant colors as usual and were unaware of the sad mist.

For as long as the Mimes could remember, every day at three o'clock Monsieur Silence, the Master Mime, has been leading the Mimes in their afternoon illusion exercises. This is the time when the Mimes practice creating illusions – the most important and exciting class in the Silent Land. In this class, the Mimes use their imaginations to share what they imagine through motion and movement – that's what Mimes do. Touching the invisible, feeling empty space, and creating a vivid picture through body language to share with each other – this is all daily practice when you live in the clouds. This is all taught with verve and passion by Monsieur Silence. Creating something out of nothing is on the agenda each and every day in Silent Land in the Sky and the Mimes really have a blast creating illusions!

Having a full and flourishing imagination is the most im-portant and respected ability for the Mimes up in the clouds.

Expressing yourself from the heart is the most esteemed. The most popular and exciting workout is "emotion aerobics" which is studied tirelessly. When doing emotion aerobics, each Mime expresses how they feel, allowing their colors to shine and flow freely. Ultimately, the Mime school's highest degree, a Doctorate in the Art of Mime, is bestowed upon those who express themselves with flair in the most glorious, far reaching and colorful way. This is a lifelong study and is the goal for each member of the Mime community.

Of course, because it is absolutely silent in Silent Land, no ever is told to "be quiet". And more so, no one is ever told to "stop expressing themselves" or to "stop flashing colors in the sky"—No, not in Silent Land! Of course, it is completely silent so no one is ever told anything at all!

What Mimes do best is express themselves in silence. In fact, each Mime, whether young or old, is expected and encouraged to express or "mime" fully and completely, and as often as they like. It is expected of each Mime that they express their own unique thoughts to their fullest ability, which at once creates wild and wonderful flourishes of colorful designs in the sky.

It is a great success and honor to have your inner expression felt, seen and shared by others, and to move onward to design new, spontaneous and unknown ideas. This large yet silent expression of feelings is most respected in Silent Land. Emotional expression and colors flying everywhere are never considered messy – they are always admired!

In fact, one time, following the birth of his granddaughter, Monsieur Silence expressed his joy so strongly that he completely changed the color of the sky, turning the entire land golden for a week! This was when Monsieur Silence was awarded the Mime Master Medal of Honor for his unbounded expression.

On this particular day, Monsieur Silence came out from the cloud entrance of the building nearby. As he strutted out, a wide smile spread across his face and all manner of colors flared above his head like a rainbow to announce his glowing presence. Yes, Monsieur Silence is the wisest and most expressive Mime in Silent Land. Greeting the Mime community, he walked toward them strong and straight and opened his arms to greet and gather all, as purple, pink, green, blue, yellow and red flashed across the sky.

He gathered the community of Mimes in the cloud playground to practice creating illusions. As he began to demonstrate, colors emanated from his body like a peacock spreading its wings, but ten times more colorful (if such a thing can be imagined).

He began creating illusions and touched an invisible wall in space. He looked at it and placed his hand out flat to touch it – and then the other hand. The wall became visible and yet, it was transparent. It was as if he touched a flat surface that already existed in space and sculpted it invisibly with his touch. And there it was! He grabbed an invisible door knob and opened the invisible door, stepping through it with ease. Then all the Mimes touched their own illusory walls and opened their invisible doors. It looked so real that it made you wonder—maybe there are unseen walls in empty space!

Chapter 2:

Mime M.I.A.

(Missing In Action)

One Mime was missing, and still nobody seemed to notice. As Fortune the Mime sat alone far beyond the colorful arch of silence, she peeked over at her peers watching and feeling very lonely. Her heart sank, heavy with sadness, which would have been clear for all to see, but she was far away and all alone. Her aura was glowing the melancholy shade of blue violet which spread out along the cloud land as a sullen, gloomy mist. She had just decided that she was going to leave the Silent Land in the Sky, forever. She felt that she just didn't fit in anymore. She rose to her feet and turned away from Silent Land, trembling inside.

Stopping and turning to look back once more, Fortune saw her Mime family and friends in the distance, practicing with Monsieur Silence. Together, they were silently touching the invisible walls in space and creating illusions in beautiful rainbows of color. She hung her head and a tear fell from her eye. She would miss her beloved home. Fortune snuck sadly away, moving towards the vast expanse of white clouds that spread out beyond into the open sky. As she tentatively stepped over the fluffy ground beyond the boundaries of Silent Land, she thought back to the moment she decided to leave...

Fortune and her fellow Mimes were working out in the mystical Studio of Creativity. Before entering the studio, each Mime shimmied and shook in order to let go of any and all colors from the day. Then, they entered through the back door, walking backwards into the Studio of Creativity to leave all thoughts and feelings outside.

Fortune shimmied and shook and yet still had a soft blue violet mist surrounding her. She twirled and jumped and spun trying everything to shake it off. She wanted to participate so much that she even tried to hide the colors! She waited until everyone was inside and then snuck in backwards, still with colors.

Once inside the studio, the real mime imagination workout started. Each Mime began to imagine ideas beyond any they had ever had before. It was getting very hot and sweaty but Monsieur Silence appeared not to notice as he demonstrated how to create the illusion of a wall. Focusing his eyes on his hands as he reached out, palms flat into the empty space, he found the wall, at first unable to move through it. He followed along the invisible wall with his hands and found a doorway and went through, shut the door and disappeared behind it.

His audience of Mimes began to practice their own versions of touching and shifting through invisible walls they built. Still blue violet, Fortune was so wrapped up in building and creating her wall that her invisible wall got bigger and thicker. In fact, soon she had built it so large that she was being pushed backwards by the wall itself. The others stopped and watched with surprise. She touched and focused on the wall so intently that the wall grew and took on a life of its own.

As Fortune's wall kept getting thicker, she was unable to break the illusion. It grew in thickness, and more walls appeared around her. She was creating an endless maze as she focused on the walls with more and more intensity. She started bumping into them. They pushed her back and she disappeared. She was now stuck between them and they began to squeeze her in until she was stuck in a box. She began to get very upset and lose control and colors flew out of the box of walls. Finally, Monsieur Silence jumped in, creating the illusion of a door in the box for Fortune to escape through.

But, when Monsieur Silence opened the door, something very strange happened…a loud noise came from inside the box! As the door opened, all could see and hear that Fortune was very upset inside the box. Fortune was sobbing **out loud** as tears rolled down her face! The absoluteness of the silence was broken! The Mimes looked on in disbelief and shock.

At that moment, all colors dissolved, leaving a shocking flash of white in their place. Sound never happened in the Silent Land. Mimes live and create in the absence of sound, so what was this? How did Fortune break the perfect silence and dissolve the color? This was impossible for a Mime!

Everyone was shocked. Fortune stood red-faced back from on

the other side of her invisible wall still sobbing loudly. She held her hands to her mouth to stop the flow of sound that had rushed out and gulped. At last there was silence again. The white flash turned to splashes of new colors of shame. The silence and new colors made Fortune feel all the more ashamed, and very alone.

Monsieur Silence came toward Fortune and held her hands. He smiled knowing that she had stepped into a new place beyond her wall that others had not yet seen. He knew she would have to explore her new experience on her own. No Mime had any experience with sound before — not even Monsieur Silence! Encouraged by Monsieur Silence, the Mimes circled Fortune and swayed slowly. As they left, each Mime felt a little bit changed by the sounds that were heard for the first time ever.

Fortune was dismayed and astonished at the sounds she had made. Yet inwardly, she felt thrilled by them and awestruck. Did she actually have a voice? No Mime had ever in Mime Time Memory— had a voice! She was confused as she left the imagination studio that day, her colors muted and unclear. But still Fortune couldn't shake the thought from her mind. She wanted to hear her voice again and to break the invisible sound barrier.

Stumbling on a cloud bump, Fortune was immediately shaken out of her memory back to the present. She stopped and took a deep breath, centering herself. But she continued walking away from Silent Land and out to the white expansive clouds beyond. Fortune was dazed. Confused and uncertain, she continued on, farther than she had ever been.

As she continued further into unknown clouds, one step at a time, suddenly her ever-silent footsteps—began to make sounds! "More sounds?" she thought. A squishing sound. Shocked and shaken that she could hear her footsteps, she stopped and looked down. Was this real? Slowly and carefully, she lifted her foot and began to tip toe as lightly as possible. But still she heard sound ... *Squish* ... *Squish* ... *Splunch* ... ever so softly at first, and growing louder and louder the further away she walked from Silent Land. Each step she made became louder and louder until she had to hold her hands over her ears, unused to sound of any kind. How strange this was. How loud she was!

She skipped three times. *Plunk* ... *Scrunch* ... *Plop!* Astounded, she continued and the patter of her steps created a musical beat. She danced to the music of her own footsteps. The louder the sound of the footsteps, the more she danced. As her hands moved away from her ears, she twirled with her arms wide open. She was entering the world of sound and she was leaving Silent Land for the first time in her life.

Excited, but also frightened, she danced and twirled creating swooshing, whooshing sounds. The cloud she was crossing began to soften and shift from the color splashes of the Silent Land to transparent white. Then, the ground beneath her feet was no longer holding her light body. She started to sink deeper with each swishy noisy step. Starting to panic, her heart pounded loudly and tears blurred her vision, causing her to trip. She fell with a loud thud, one foot sinking through the cloud beneath her. As she tried to grab hold and pull herself up, the other foot became stuck and she lost her balance again, this time causing her to lurch right over the edge of the cloud!

She grasped the edge of the cloud -- the only thing stopping her from falling. Hanging by one hand in the open air, Fortune was dangling dangerously off the edge of the cloud! Yet, she was wide eyed and amazed as she hung there, for she could see the world below her.

Way down below, there was a lush green forest. And still further away in the distance there was a big city. As her ears adjusted, sounds rose up toward her from the forest. The swoosh of trees, the tweets of birds, the hum of crickets from the forest and honking horns, rumbling engines, and the strange mechanical noises from the city – all these sounds she had never experienced before. To Fortune, these sounds were like menacing strangers she was never supposed to meet. Would she was risk everything to find them and meet face to face?

Frightened, she realized she wanted nothing to do with the noisy world below, and she decided leaving the Silent Land she knew and loved was not a good idea at all. She struggled to drag herself up and rested her elbows on the edge of the cloud. She was out of breathe and her legs still dangled in mid air. She gazed back in the direction of Silent Land, and watched with new eyes as way in the distance,

Monsieur Silence and the Mimes moved as one under the rainbow in silence, and different colors flashed everywhere.

"Which way should I go?" she thought, very distraught. Looking down, she suddenly slipped a few inches. Panicking, she kicked her leg up and over and finally pulled herself back onto the cloudbank.

Chapter 3:

A Singing Mime?!

She lay there, her heart was beating wildly and she was huffing and puffing and trying to catch her breath. "Was there nothing she could do right?" she thought. Slowly recovering, she got up and ran toward safer more colorful clouds. She hid behind a fluffy cloud bump, took a deep breath, opened her mouth, and tried to make a sound. Nothing. Silence. And colors … many wonderful colors. The colors were deep and flowing. She knew that she was expressing a new thought and a new desire with new and brighter colors. She loved the colors all around. And it was obvious that the colors disappeared with sound.

But she still wanted to speak… even more than that… She wanted to…. *sing*…yes, sing… sing the silent words out loud! To sing out loud and radiate even more colors with sound - all together and at the same time! To bash the barrier of silence! But, there has never been a singing Mime!

Fortune wished silently and as she wished she heard a silent song from deep within:

Silently searching for my voice
So much to say, my words, my choice
And when I sing,
You'll hear every word,
That is so, That is so.

I'll sing "I'm happy to be me!"
and I'll tell you anything you want to hear,
But silence covers me,
like leaves on a tree,
That is so, Oh that is so.

The Sound Barrier Bash,
The Sound Barrier Bash,
Oh I'd like to fly the speed of light and crash
Through the wall,
Where I can find my voice,

You'll hear me laugh,
You'll hear me sing,
You'll see me talking to everything.
From now on I vow to search
For my voice, my voice.
The Sound Barrier Bash,
The Sound Barrier Bash,

Oh I'd like to fly the speed of light and crash
through the wall,
where I can find my voice.

Fortune's eyes were now very wide and lit up. She *heard* the silent song. Yes, it was a *silent* song but she could hear it loud and clear. She thought, "I don't belong in Silent Land anymore"…and she was certain of this. She had to find her voice and sing out loud. How could she find the courage to leave the clouds and go to such a strange and noisy place as Earth, so far below?

Then it hit her. "Maybe… just maybe ", she wondered, "Maybe Monsieur Silence had shown her the way!" She remembered what happened in the clouds a few days before …

Monsieur Silence was again giving a demonstration of his great skills before eager Mimes. This time he was showing them one of the most beautiful illusions of them all — to fly like a bird.

Monsieur Silence asked all the Mimes to line up in a 'V' shape on the field of clouds. As they moved their arms and bodies up and down, all together, they, suddenly felt the sensation and began to look like a flock of birds in formation, winging and soaring majestically through the air. Fortune lost herself in the sensation and motion of flying.

Remembering the feeling of flight, Fortune was inspired and energized. She now knew what to do! She would fly to noisy Earth to find her voice. With joy, she jumped up and ran at full speed toward the edge of the cloud. With a deep breath she opened her arms wide, lifted her heart, and before she had a chance to regret her decision,

she leaped ...

Chapter 4:

The First Encounter

Falling, falling, spinning and falling. She held out her arms and flew like Monsieur Silence had taught her, while whirling spiraling rainbows all around her slowed down her fall. She landed with a soft thud and bounced on deep soft grass, rolling down a hill before coming to a stop. With her arms out and lying face down, she lay there for a while listening to her heart beat loudly against the earth, so loud and strange. This loud thumping of her heart was so strong it seemed to be shaking the ground.

Fortune slowly sat up, looking around at this new world. She felt the earthy dirt beneath her and was surrounded on all sides by high grass. She noticed there were no more swirling colors in the sky. "Oh no, what have I done!" she thought.

Everything was so noisy and new – the wind and birds and rustling of the trees. Fortune peeked her head above the long grass and looked around, again clutching her ears to block out the strange sounds of the unfamiliar forest. She peered cautiously all around amazed at where she found herself. She touched the ground and it felt solid and warm. She felt a sense of being grounded which she had never felt before.

As she looked in the distance there was noise and lights and she could see a city skyline with cars speeding on the streets and smoke stacks billowing with gray swirling smoke. Confused and frightened, she turned and ran the other way, deep into the forest.

Fortune ran clumsily. She wasn't used to being on solid ground, so her feet felt heavy as she ran through the brush and trees. Soon, her steps lightened as she started to adjust to gravity and solid ground. Finally, she began to run with ease. That is, until she heard a very loud crash that stopped her in her tracks. She dove to safety behind a willow tree, taking cover from the unseen cause of the crash. The noise was followed by a magnificent roar.

"What was that?!" she thought. She hid behind the trunk of the willow tree, terrified! All alone on Earth in a colorless sky, she stood shaking.

Slowly, oh so slowly, she parted the hanging willow branches through the leaves ... and she saw him ... a huge lion. He was stomping around strangely. He turned his head quickly and with a sharp stop he counted, "A one, a two and a one two three and a one, a two and a one two three...turn stop," he roared to the beat. Then with a big grin, he stepped out and bowed ... and forgetting to look down, he tripped on a gnarled tree trunk and fell flat on his face! Roaring even louder, he jumped awkwardly back to his feet, accidentally hitting the nest of a poor little bird family with his outstretched paw. The birds flew frantically away in a flurry, chirping loudly, very upset as their nest flew to pieces. "Watch out, watch out, watch out!" the birds all screeched, flying every which way.

Trying in vain to pick up the pieces of the nest, the lion trudged on a beautiful rose, squashing it into the dirt of the forest floor. He picked it up but it was crushed. Feeling terrible about his clumsiness, he turned around to walk away, but as he did so his long tail smacked a rabbit square in the face. Ouch!

And Fortune could hear all the creatures of the forest start to whisper and gossip about the lion. "Watch out! Phil the lion will stomp on your mole hole and cause an avalanche in your cave. He'll ruin your winter nap or whack your nest off the branch with his tail and send it flying. He's out of control!" they said. Far from a big strong confident quick stepping lion, he felt like a clumsy beast. He lay down on his back, covered his eyes with his paws and went to sleep. Fortune watched him as she hid behind the tree.

Growing in courage, as Phil the lion slept, Fortune tiptoed forward in his direction. She marveled at his huge furry paws and feet. She curiously stepped out of hiding as Phil began to release thunderous snores so loud she quickly held her ears as tight as she could.

There was Phil in a deep sleep with a dream cloud hovering above his head! He was dreaming about what he always dreamed about; being a world famous tango dancer wearing a tuxedo on Broadway! The many animals and birds and fish in the dream all cheered and clapped as Phil danced. A dreamy eyed rabbit swooned and fainted as she watched him with adoration. The animals chirped and squeaked and growled and gurgled singing to the beat...

There is a place where you can go
Where you can be what you want to be,
Do what you want to do,
Anytime... anywhere.

It's a place where you can laugh
And dance and sing,
It's all you have to do.

Come with us to find your dream,
No matter how wild it may seem,
Take a step towards your desire,
It shapes your life and lights your fire.

You are special just as you are,
Living your dream makes you a star.
Come, come with us,
Follow your dream,
No matter how strange it may seem.
Believe in yourself,
Your secrets matter,

Take big steps up life's great ladder.
Do the things you really love,
Life will be filled with the love you give.

Fortune knew exactly what Phil was dreaming about because she could see it all playing out in the dream cloud above his head. Phil was so very handsome as he danced the tango gracefully and regally in his dream. His chest held high, he smiled and his roar was confident yet gentle as the animals of the forest applauded his amazing moves. He stepped and turned with his head held high.

Fortune watched with wide eyes and smiled. She felt herself swooning a bit and was quite taken with the dancing lion.

Delighted and amazed and touched by the lion's dream, Fortune reached out to touch the dream cloud with her finger. Her finger touched the cloud and the touch caused it to wobble like a soap bubble! Then it wobbled more and more and so much it looked like it was about it burst.

"Oh no!" she thought, looking down at the very large sleeping lion. Phil's dream was changing as it wobbled. As he danced, Phil was now desperately trying to keep his balance in the wobbly cloud and his audience began to disperse. He then lost his balance, battling with gravity, and fell on the Broadway stage! Getting up, he looked straight out of his dream cloud and locked eyes with Fortune. With that, Phil the lion awoke from his slumber.

"Ahhhhhhhhhhhh!" Phil roared.

Fortune jumped and ran – her arms in the air. Phil gave chase as both ran out from beneath the willow tree, each terrified in equal measure, like a mouse up against an elephant. Running around the tree in opposite directions, they bumped right into each other and fell to the ground. Suddenly Phil saw that Fortune was staring at something above his head. His dream cloud was still hanging in the air!

His whiskered cheeks turned red and he got up and ran for cover beneath the willow tree once more, embarrassed that someone had seen his secret dream.

"Oh no! , Phil said to himself horrified, " Please no! She didn't see it. I don't know what she saw, but I hope she didn't see what she saw!"

Fortune, seeing his dream very clearly, wanted to let Phil know how great she thought he was as he danced the tango in his dream. She went looking for him behind the tree trunk. Silently, she pointed to the dream cloud and smiled. But Phil was simply frozen with shame. Fortune, still enamored with the dream watched as the cloud started floating away. She looked at Phil, tilted her head in wonder and pointed to the dream cloud encouraging him to go after it. But Phil looked the other way trying to avoid her. So Fortune tried to catch the cloud herself, but she was too small to reach it as it floated upwards into the sky.

"I'm gonna run like crazy, I just gotta get out of here. I'll just slip out of here and then I'll be gone," Phil said to himself knowing his oh-so-hidden dream was exposed. He tried in vain to tip-toe away quietly, but the more he tried to be silent, the louder the sound that each footstep made.

Chapter 5:

Who is Who?

Fortune followed Phil close behind. She delicately danced to the beat as she followed, imitating the dance moves Phil had done with the animals. A one, a two, a one- two- three. Phil could hear her footsteps behind him. At first he pretended not to notice, then suddenly he twirled on his heel and turned to face Fortune with an angry scowl and a fearsome growl. To his surprise and dismay, Fortune was not scared at all, and as he turned to walk away, she proceeded to dance to the beat following right behind him once again.

Visibly growing more aggravated by the minute, Phil turned back to face her again. "You go where you gotta go," he said pointing at her. And he pointed his paw towards his own chest, "and I'll go where I gotta go."

Fortune simply continued to mimic every move her new buddy made pointing both ways and getting her arms twisted around each other.

Phil looked at her with complete surprise. "Okay, I'm gonna cover my eyes and when I open then, vamoose! You'd better be gone if you know what's good for you." He was trying his best to sound very gruff and serious. He opened his eyes to find Fortune still there and still matching his every move with a smile.

Suddenly, just as his confusion was at its peak, the birds, still fixing their nest, flew into the clearing and danced around their heads chirping in unison:

I am you, You are me,
Who is who, Who are we?
Foot to foot, Knee to knee,
Eye to eye, Together we see.

"Yeah, yeah, yeah...", said Phil responding sarcastically to the birds with his hands on his hips. Fortune also put her hands on her hips silently expressing with the exact sarcastic body language as Phil.

Then from the nearby brook the shiny-scaled fish begin to jump splash and gurgle seeing their reflections in the water:

I feel this way,
You feel that way,
is anyone right and is anyone wrong?
We all dance to the mirror song.

Then all the animals in different sounds from deep in the

forest said all together:

One to one, two together
Blending into one another
dancing closely, you and me
Moving simultaneously.

The animals went flying and scurrying and swimming away. Phil crossed his arms and frowned a big frown. Again Fortune imitated him. She looked so funny trying to make herself look like a big angry lion that Phil couldn't help himself, and he let out a bellowing laugh.

"Can you be serious? Are you for real?" he said, feeling self-conscious and not knowing what else to say, having gone from happy to sad to angry and back again in a matter of moments.

Fortune nodded her head to say that yes, she was indeed for real.

"Well, try this then", said Phil finally playing back... he did a few rumba steps roaring, "One two three and a one two three." Fortune tried to follow and they rumbaed together out from under the trees and up onto the well-worn spot the creatures of the forest called the Grassy Knoll. "Not bad!" he said. "OK then! How about this!" He did the Cha-cha-cha, "One, two and cha-cha-cha". They pranced and they danced around together as all the animals looked on. They danced and danced.

Shimmying their shoulders with the salsa, both of them were laughing and sweating, Fortune silently with a glowing smile. Phil was laughing and roaring so loudly he had to catch himself. Phil thought he saw colors flying around Fortune as she daintily shimmied. He stopped for a moment and looked seeing colors swirling all around her. Not sure, he closed his eyes and shook his head. When he opened his eyes, the colors had disappeared.

With his pride and confusion getting the better of him, Phil stood up straight and brushed himself off, with dust, leaves and grass flying in all directions. "Who are you anyway?" he asked Fortune.

Fortune stood back, twirled gracefully on the spot and bowed before Phil. Then she gestured towards him, asking him in her silent and polite way who he was.

"Oh. Well, I'm, um … Phillip," he stuttered in response more politely than usual. "Yeah, but they call me Phil…Phil the Lion." In a vain attempt to be as graceful as Fortune, he twirled twice on his heels, making himself dizzy. As he lost his balance and his long tail came back around it hit Fortune, knocking her to the ground in an instant. "Oh no, I'm so sorry!" bellowed Phil, mortified at his return to clumsiness.

Fortune lay on the ground in a slight daze, rubbing her head.

"Let me help you. Come on up," Phil said as he dragged Fortune to her feet. Fortune stood upright, regaining her composure.

"I'm sorry. I didn't mean it. I'm this clumsy, big, can't-do-anything-right-in-the-world…beast," Phil cried. "I'm a beast. That's what I am. I'm nothing but an oversized beast." He sat down on a nearby rock, his expression becoming more and more glum with each passing moment. Finally, tears began to trickle down his cheek. "I don't have any friends. You can't be my friend you know. I'll wind up knocking you all over the place and not even knowing that I did it."

Fortune frowned at him, showing her disagreement.

"Well, tell me then, how am I going to be your friend?" said Phil.

Fortune reached out to Phil and took his huge paw in her hand. Phil didn't know it yet, but she understood perfectly well how he felt.

"I don't have any friends. Everybody's afraid of me because they're supposed to be afraid of me and it's not fair! I don't do what I do to scare anyone. I'm just a big guy, but they call me a beast! A beast!" Phil let out a huge rasping roar as he continued, "I think I'm the nicest beast around! I am! I really am!"

Phil had his back to Fortune by now, and his head was in his hands as he paced back and forth. He failed to notice his roar had knocked the light Mime off her feet again! "I don't know what I'm gonna do." Phil exclaimed. By now he was completely overcome with emotion, and he roared sadly, telling his secret to Fortune .....

It stinks to be such a big klutzy guy,
My tail will womp you right square in the eye
And if I sneeze there'll be WOW what a breeze,
A breeze that'll blow you right out of the trees.

I wish I was as tiny as a flea,
It sure stinks to be a big guy like me!
I wish I could sail away out to the sea,
It stinks to be a big guy like me!

If you hear me roar or you listen to me snore
With my big curly head up against a tree,
You'll know it's hard, it's really, really hard
To make good friends in your own back yard.

I wish I was as tiny as a flea,
It sure stinks to be a big guy like me!

Collapsing in a combination of despair and exhaustion, Phil slumped cross-legged to the floor, staring blankly into the darkness of the thickening forest.

"I wish I was the size of a midget gnat or something," he muttered to himself.

.

Chapter 6:

You Gotta Believe!

Fortune sat next to Phil on the forest floor. She wanted to help him understand that she understood what he was feeling.

"Go away. Will you please? I'm a beast. You don't wanna know me," he protested, trying to hide his tears as he began to sob quietly. Then he roared and sobbed loudly.

Fortune patted his back to comfort him. For a moment she thought long and hard about what she could do to cheer him up. She saw the tears in his big eyes and she began to pull something invisible but very long from her sleeve, like a magician would with a handkerchief. Slowly colors began to appear in the air — all the colors of the rainbow and more.

Fortune offered the mystical handkerchief to Phil, who accepted it graciously and used it to wipe the tears from his crying eyes. But tears kept falling from Phil's eyes, so Fortune kept handing the handkerchief to him. She kept pulling the endlessly long handkerchief out for him, as tears continued to flow. Phil's tears were so huge that they caused a raincloud above them both and it began to rain heavily.

"I'm really just a nice guy. I don't bother no one. All I wanna be is a tango dancer. I don't wanna be king of the jungle or nothin." Phil sobbed, and the forest began to flood from his tears. Water gushed everywhere from Phil's eyes and from the rain clouds.¯

Fortune kept pulling the continuous colorful kaleidoscope handkerchief out of her sleeve and handed more and more of it to Phil as he wiped his big eyes. It seemed like forever, but Phil finally looked up and noticed the endless stream of color getting bigger next to him.

When Phil finally looked up, he took a big breath and said "Wow!" as his tears stopped. He smiled and looked at Fortune quizzically and then with wonder at the seemingly endless handkerchief. And then the handkerchief disappeared.

The rain was still falling from the cloud of tears above. Fortune, trying to avoid getting soaked, mimed the action of opening an umbrella. Holding it above both of their heads, they were sheltered from the rain. Phil looked up and saw nothing there. The umbrella was invisible but the rain was not touching them. And then very slowly it actually appeared! The bright red umbrella was sheltering them from the gushing rain of sadness!

"Aaaaaachooooo!" Phil sneezed the loudest sneeze Fortune had ever heard causing the umbrella and Fortune to fly up into the air! Fortune motioned anxiously for Phil to help her before she got swept up and lost in the wind. He jumped high, reached up and just managed to grab her foot before she was blown out of reach. She smiled gratefully; the rain stopped as suddenly as it had begun.

Fortune, now laughing silently, started to dance with the umbrella, splashing with each dance step. Phil's smile widened – a sight Fortune was so glad to see. She continued to prance and twirl and splash, carefree and joyfully. Phil started to laugh again loudly, only this time he wasn't embarrassed. He couldn't stop smiling.

"Ya know, you sure are different!" Phil said laughing. She closed her umbrella and it disappeared, just like the rainbow handkerchief and Phil's tears and sadness. Pooof, Gone! The sun slowly came out from behind the scary gray clouds, shining brightly and illuminating both of them as they basked in the warmth.

"I guess things ain't that bad after all, huh?" Phil shrugged looking up at the now clear sky.

Fortune responded by pointing to the glorious Sun, whose rays had by now managed to erase any evidence of the rainfall that had threatened to overcome them only a short time before.

"It always comes out eventually, doesn't it?" he said, pondering over why he had allowed himself to become so consumed by despair. "Things really ain't that bad are they?"

Realizing she had finally made him understand that she was there for him, Fortune smiled back at Phil and nodded and motioned, as if to say "they sure ain't!"

Fully recovered by now, Phil felt a new feeling swell within him, a feeling of possibility, of hope. "Ya gotta believe," he began to say. "Ya just gotta believe."

Fortune pumped her fist in a "right on!" motion, encouraging Phil to keep thinking the way he was thinking.

"And ya gotta be strong!" continued Phil. "And tough! And rough! And all that stuff, ya gotta do it all if you wanna be good enough! Right?"

She nodded – he knew she wanted to shout "right!" in agreement.

"Put 'er there," Phil said, extending his paw. They shook hands and Fortune was thrown up in the air by Phil's power. But she just laughed silently and Phil, realizing she was a keep-er, hugged her tight.

"I got a pal! This is it. I got a companion to go with me through thick and thin, to give me advice. A sounding board! A real life, real live buddy!"

Fortune struggled to catch her breath under the weight of Phil's embrace, but she didn't have the heart to interrupt him on this most joyous of occasions for the lion, when he was finally happy after so much sadness and loneliness.

"A buddy to brainstorm with!" Phil went on, this time hitting poor Fortune with his tail. Yes, again! He didn't even notice, as he continued his monologue of happiness; "An ami-go! Someone to go after that star! After that dream! A partner!" Eventually he noticed her absence, but in his effort to locate her he swung around too fast, hitting her with his tail again!

"Hey, there you are, come here!" he said, oblivious to the trouble he was putting her through. "What are you doing down there, silly!" He helped her up and placed his arm over her shoulder.

"Do you know what I wanna do, what I wanna be, who I gotta be? Do ya? I gotta be a tango dancer!" he told her. "But I get to a certain point and then I blow it. I need that 'oomph!'", you know what I mean? Hey, what did you say your name was again?"

She motioned in such a way as to imply that she didn't say. She took his paw and placed it over her heart, and with that movement she showed him that she would be his friend no matter what. Phil no longer felt so inquisitive; he was just satisfied and happy. Together they would march on to success and victory!

It seemed like nothing could bring Phil down from the cloud of joy he was riding. "Yeah! We're gonna do it. I'm gonna get a tuxedo and everything... Wait a minute." Something clicked in his brain and he finally realized it. "You don't speak, do ya?"

Fortune shook her head, feeling a growing sense of insecurity about her silence. It made her sad. Now it was Phil's turn to be there for her, his newfound friend.

"I understand what you're saying but you're not saying nothin'!" he exclaimed. "Hey! How do ya speak... so... so softly?"

Fortune placed her hand on his heart then his on hers. She immediately made him understand without words, just like she had done before.

"Wow. I feel like... I feel like I can do anything. And like I can tell you anything! It's amazing!" he said. Fortune motioned with her head as if to say "Yes! Yes! You can tell me anything at all!"

Chapter 7:
Pals

Phil knew that he had to keep his dream alive, and that his new friend Fortune – though he didn't even know that was her name – was the only one who could help him do this. "I have to dream to know what I want," he said, turning to look into her eyes.

She once again pointed to the sun glowing far up in the sky, and he knew immediately that she understood. She always seemed to understand. With overwhelming joy he sang loudly and she danced to his song:

I hoped one day
Someone would say
I really want to be with you,

Just you - just as you are,
You got yourself a Pal!

They'll never mess around
And leave you when you're down,
Together you'll laugh and cry and play.
You got yourself a Pal!

You may not be a pretty sight that day
But they're there with you anyway
And they'll sit with you, even in the muck.
You got yourself a Pal!

As he roared happily, the animals of the forest reappeared and joined in. Fortune danced and smiled from ear to ear as she watched them tweet, roar, gurgle and chirp together:

So ya gotta wait and see,
Keep your eyes open wide,
Lay your heart out on the floor
And maybe, just maybe
You'll find a
Bonafide,
Certified,
Bestified,
You've got yourself a Pal!

If one day you find
You've messed up big time
Or you feel that you're just in the way,

You'll hear a voice say you've got a friend in me!
You've got yourself a pal!

Time will pass and
You'll get your show back on the road.
It's OK they'll say, whatever you did.
I'm by you through thick and thin
You got yourself a pal!
A bonafide,
Certified,
Qualified,
Bestified
PAL!

Phil closed his song with a huge majestic roar and the animals scurried off to their homes. He and Fortune – who had been dancing all the while – fell to the grassy ground laughing. Exhausted, but still full of joy, they both fell into the sweet silence of sleep.

Waking again, Fortune thought her memory was deceiving her – had Phil the lion just serenaded her and called her his pal?! Indeed he had! She was so excited because now she had found a friend too and that was a wonderful feeling. She shook Phil back to reality from what was, no doubt, another colorful dream and reached over to him, tagging him "it!" before silently slipping away with a huge grin on her face.

Phil jumped to his fluffy feet and was soon in hot pursuit. "I'm gonna get ya!" he half roared, half laughed. They made a dizzy trail throughout the trees until Phil finally caught up with the spritely Mime. "Tag!" With that Phil ran off into the depths of the forest, with Fortune hot on his heels.

After running and running and running, the unlikely pair eventually emerged from the thick forest and into a clearing where they marveled at the beauty of the woodland in the daylight. But this wasn't the only thing that stopped them in their tracks. Thinking that their ears were deceiving them, they could hear tango music in the distance. Suddenly it dawned on them - it was Phil's dream cloud!

Fortune smiled and turned to Phil. She gestured excitedly to him as if to say "There it is! There it is!"

Fortune continued to nudge him, suggesting that they should go get it. She was worried for a second that Phil was going to get embarrassed again.

But then Phil pronounced with vigor, "Yeah, let's do it!"

Chapter 8:

Following the Dream

L ike two mismatched spies, they crept up on the floating dream cloud as slowly as they could. But with every step, the cloud moved a step further away. Not one to be outwitted, Fortune jumped into a sudden run and leaped forward to grab the dream cloud. But she missed again, falling to the ground as the cloud evaded her grasp and swished off into the distance.

As he helped Fortune to her feet, Phil felt a glint of sadness hit him as the sound of the tango music he loved faded. But he wasn't about to give up. "Hey, buddy, I don't think anyone can grab it but me", he whispered half to himself and half out loud. Fortune nodded in agreement. Together they walked toward the cloud. As their determination and resolve grew, that walk turned into a jog, and then that jog turned into a brisk run.

"Wait, wait, wait!" Phil skidded to a halt out of the blue. Fortune could almost see the light bulb flicker into life above his head. "Let me try and get it this way," he said, as Fortune watched on with growing curiosity.

Phil stood still for a moment, before inhaling one of the biggest breaths of air that Fortune had ever seen, sucking branches, twigs, flowers and grass from the ground and trees. The pull was so great that Fortune had to hold tightly to a tree to stop herself from being sucked in with the rest of the forest. But Phil grew lightheaded from the exertion, and was about to stop just as a huge, gnarled tree stump came loose from the earth and flew at him, hitting him smack in the face! Fortune ran to help her friend, slapping his cheeks to try and finally bringing him back to consciousness.

"I'm ok. I'm ok," said Phil, though he was clearly still in a daze. Fortune slumped down on the ground next to him. They watched as the cloud floated back into view for a mocking minute, and then away again, out of sight.

"Bummer. Bummer, bummer, bummer," Phil mumbled almost incoherently. Feeling sad for him, Fortune picked a 'mime flower' from the ground and held it out for Phil, but he wouldn't take it. "That ain't a real flower," he scoffed. "You sure are strange!" "I don't think I'm cut out to be a dreamer, you know," Phil suggested, in a resigned tone. But Fortune wasn't willing to let him start feeling sorry for himself again, and she motioned to him to stop thinking such thoughts. She put the invisible flower into his paw, whether he wanted it or not. Grumpy now, Phil mimed throwing it away. Fortune ran to pick up the invisible flower, but as she held it up, it wilted in her hand. She quickly put it back into the ground and mimed the act of watering it.

Then another unexpected thing happened; a real flower sprouted up out of the ground where Fortune stood. Phil rubbed his eyes in disbelief. But somehow this wasn't enough to inspire him, not yet anyway.

"No, no, no. I can't follow that dream cloud. I just don't.... I don't even know where it is now anyway," he moaned. Fortune wasn't giving up on him just yet though. Thinking on her feet as always, she climbed a tree to use as a lookout post. Soon, in the distance, Fortune saw the dream cloud floating in a ray of sunlight. Far away it was drifting calmly. From the top of the tree, she motioned to Phil that she had spotted the cloud.

"Get outta here. Where?"

She waved for Phil to hurry and follow her up the tree. There was no time for doubt or skepticism!

"Way up there?" he hesitated. "Aww, here goes nothin' I guess." He climbed awkwardly up to the top of the tree, where he joined Fortune at her lookout post. She pointed in the direction of his dream cloud and Phil soon spotted it for himself. By now it was floating ominously over the edge of a cliff.

"Yikes," Phil said. "I think it's too dangerous to go after that dream. I'm gettin' down from here." He began to clamber down the tree as awkwardly as he had climbed up it. "I'm history. I can't do this!" he kept saying. But as he was halfway down the tree, branches started to bend under his weight, in turn causing the whole tree to bend over. The large branch under Phil's foot finally broke and he fell to the ground. He hit the leafy ground with such a smack that it made the entire forest shake. Discouraged, he lay on the ground covering his eyes, Fortune grabbed onto another branch and dangled delicately in the air before dropping lightly down to the ground.

Both friends looked at each other in doubting silence. It was obvious they were both wondering whether or not they should continue. But, finding her resolve again, Fortune put out her hand. Phil obligingly reached for it and got up to his feet again. Paw in hand, hand in paw, they marched off at a steady pace toward the cliff.

When they got to the edge, the cloud was still there, floating just out of reach. Another idea jumped into Phil's head, and he motioned for Fortune to climb on his back. She jumped up onto his shoulders, and together they tried reaching for the cloud again.

"I can't reach it," Phil said.

Fortune nodded yes you can insisting and getting her point across in silence by tugging on his neck.

"I can't."

She started to jump up and down pointing and directing him to keep trying to catch his dream.

"I can't!" Frustrated, Phil took Fortune down from his shoulders. "No no no. Just... why don't you go find another friend?"

Fortune looked at him blankly. She was shocked and sad. *Because I'll never be able to,* she thought to herself. Devastated, Fortune walked away.

"Oh, no no no. Wait."

But she kept walking, so Phil followed. "Wait a minute now. You said you were gonna be my friend, and you said you were gonna help me, and you said together we were gonna catch my dream!"

She turned and stared at him, tilting her head quizzically. She was more than a bit exasperated and very annoyed with him now.

"Ok. Actually you didn't say nothin'," Phil admitted. As she crossed her arms and tapped her foot, Phil bowed his head in shame. "What a mope I am, huh?"

Fortune was hurt but refused to show it for a moment longer, and so she stepped forward and posed like a tango dancer, motioning for him to do the same.

"Aaaall right then." He slowly stepped forward and assumed the same pose, and the tango music drifted back into earshot as suddenly as it had earlier drifted out. Fortune took a step. Phil followed. The process continued until a fully fledged tango had developed!

Phil soon became overly enthusiastic and he ran off on his own, dancing and singing with a funny Spanish accent. "I can kick. And leap. Que bueno!! And twirl in the air!" Unknowingly, he was knocking down trees, kicking up flowers, as well as drilling huge holes in the ground with each twirl. "Bailamos, shall we dance? Si! Si! I'm dancing all over the place. Aha si, si." Lagging behind her over-eager student, Fortune followed as close as she could, trying her best to fix the damage Phil was unwittingly causing.

The music came to an end just as Phil fell into a thorny bush whereupon he was attacked by its prickles. "Oouuchh!", he yelled.

Rolling her eyes, Fortune pulled the little thorns out of his backside.

"What a pal, what a pal, what a pal!" Phil shouted excitedly. "I'm gonna dance." And with that he ran off yet again. The wind could be heard starting to whirl as Phil twirled wildly into the forest, destroying pretty much everything in his path. Fortune followed looking up.

Chapter 9:

The Tornado

Phil's twirling had created a spiraling wind that transformed into a dark tornado with its own menacing silhouette and facial features above him. Fortune hung onto a tree for safety. She watched as Phil's dream cloud was blown far away into the distance, not that he noticed himself.

Birds and moles and squirrels and mice flew and ran and hid and burrowed saying:

You are stirring things up and creating a mess!
Your dream is making everyone stress!
Everything is changing! Stop right now!
Your dancing is causing things to fly around!
Things were normal once and now they're not,
You've got us in an awful spot!

Your dancing is causing so much change,
Our lives messed up and rearranged.

Before she knew it, the Tornado had whipped Fortune from her tree and she flew helplessly through the air, circling towards its dark center.

Meanwhile the Tornado was creating destruction wherever it touched down throughout the forest. Phil was now completely controlled by the whirling wind, a wind he had created.

"Help!!!" Phil and Fortune grabbed onto each other, and they spun around and around and around within it. Suddenly they heard a voice come from within the swirling cloud. "You dancing fool. You've turned your big dream into a nightmare! Hahaha!"

Phil tried his best to stand tall and be brave against the punishing wind as Fortune struggled behind him. "Oh, yeah?!" Phil proclaimed defiantly. The Tornado began to spin Phil and Fortune ever more violently, tossing them around like rag dolls. The Tornado continued to laugh cynically at their plight.

"Oh no! What have I done?! " Phil asked in vain.

Inside the Tornado, Phil and Fortune were being tossed like rag dolls. Birds, animals, trees, leaves and rocks were also being hurled around by the powerful force of nature.

"You want to be a world famous tango dancer? Look at those huge paws. And you're too clumsy to boot!" The Tornado belted out thunderous laugh after thunderous laugh. "You're clumsy and too big and you always will be! How dare you think such things! Dance then! Go ahead dance – beast!"

Go ahead and dance beast!
Go ahead and dream.

Your head is in the clouds.
It has always been!

Go ahead and dance beast.
Ha! Your dream is just a joke.
You're ugly and clumsy and too big.
You make me laugh until I choke!

You dancing fool,
Your life's gone wrong
You think you'll fit right in,
But just look around.
You can't make dreams real
You'll never dance or win!
AH ha ha!
A dream cannot be real!
Go ahead – dream big – dance faster!
Follow your silly dream cloud beast.
It can only end in disaster.

Phil managed to hold onto a tree, and Fortune clung onto his tail. "I really don't think this dream thing is working out," he said.

Fortune shook her head from side to side in response. "No." And with that Fortune lost her grip on Phil's tail and was blown up against a tree. There she found a bird's nest with eggs in it. Before the eggs were swept out into the storm Fortune grabbed them. As she did, one cracked and a little chick shrieked with fright as it was blown into the breast of the struggling Mother Bird. Mother Bird caught her chick and the rest of her eggs and they were all blown away together just before the nest was blown apart and destroyed, with remnants hitting Fortune in the face.

Phil spun faster and faster as he dropped lower and lower toward the base of the Tornado. The Tornado continued to laugh, "Your head is in the clouds, you beast. There is no hope. You're wasting your time."

"I started you – you big whirlwind - and I can stop you!" Phil roared.

Phil's big feet were sticking out as he spun. He focused downward and started spinning down, down, down. Soon he had reached the base of the Tornado, still spinning in one perfect motion. He planted his feet in the dirt like a corkscrew still spinning. As his big feet went deeper into the ground, he was holding back the swirl of the tornado! It was causing the Tornado to slow down.

"What are you doing? Hey Stop!" said the Tornado, sounding shaky and insecure for the first time.

Phil's feet dug deeper and deeper into the dirt, like a drill, as he continued to twirl.

"Hey Lion! Stop! Stop! Move your feet!" the Tornado pleaded as its dark spinning mass got smaller and smaller. "Hey Lion, I didn't mean it. You can dance. Dance now! Move your feet!" But Phil held his feet strong in the earth. Phil was going deeper and deeper into the mud and holding the wind back. The Tornado finally faltered with a loud " ahhhhhh". It shrank and softened into a sweet gentle breeze.

Fortune fell gently from the sky on the breeze with a swoosh and landed ker- plunk next to Phil who was buried up to his arm paws in the mud. The sound of the wind left the forest.

The aftermath of the Tornado wasn't pretty, that's for sure. The forest was in complete shambles. It looked darker and grayer than it ever had before. Worst of all, it was eerily quiet, incomparable to the vibrant land of chirping birds and scurrying squirrels that it had been only a short while before. The animals were all away in hiding, fearing for their lives and the lives of their young ones.

Phil was stuck so far into the mud that it took Fortune an hour to dig him out. After, Phil sat among the tree stumps and upturned earth, trying to piece a bird's nest back together. Fortune was kneeling in front of a small campfire, warming her hands. Her face was dirty, her clothes were disheveled and her hair was a mess. But she was okay. The sun had yet to show its face again.

"This following my dream idea of yours — it just ain't workin'," Phil said. "Man! This is insane. The forest is a mess. I'm falling out of trees and causing tornadoes. And worst of all I've hurt all the animals, ruined their homes… And you, you're a mess too — because of me!"

Phil turned away from Fortune, not realizing that he had mistakenly stuck his tail and rear end straight into the fire. "I hate me! I'm just too big to dance, plain and simple," he whined. "Who needs this? You should have left me sleeping. I was happy and not botherin' nobody."

Suddenly Phil's tail started to smoke. Just as the smell reached his nostrils and he was beginning to puzzle over its origins, the whole thing erupted into flames.

"Aaaaahh!" He jumped and ran around in circles with the flame whooshing from his tail in a bright orange swoop of light every time he swung it. "Put it out! Put it out! Put it ooooout!" wailed Phil.

Fortune finally managed to put the fire out. Phil leaned against a tree, relieved and exhausted. "Okay. This is it. I can't do this anymore. My tail is burnt. I... I..." Lost for words, he continued to pace around, before gathering up a huge pile of leaves to sleep on.

"This is the ultimate worst," Phil said, finding his voice. "A bum tail on a lion is the end! You ever see a lion with a bum tail? Fortune shook her head to say "no" but Phil wasn't looking at her. He was too wrapped up in himself and his own damaged pride. "Huh? Did ya? Did ya? What's that you say? Would ya speak up?!" he said, taunting her silence on purpose. She shook her head again then bowed it in sadness and Fortune's heart sank.

"I'm going to sleep," Phil growled as he lay down. "Ouch! Oooh that hurts," he exclaimed, rubbing his burnt backside. "Grrrrrr, good night!"

Chapter 10:

The Aftermath

Fortune motioned to say "good night" back to him but he had turned away. She walked over to the outside of their makeshift camp and laid down. A few solitary tear drops fell from her eyes. She wiped them away and fell asleep.

As another night became day, the fire smoldered and Fortune lay sleeping. For a while the Forest was still gray, colorless and quiet. But then came the sun, shining a very bright ray of light into Phil's eyes, waking him right up. To his sleepy surprise, the dream cloud floated above him, bobbing over and back from the shade into the light. Shielding his eyes, Phil looked up and saw the dream cloud floating across the path of the sun, blocking the ray of light that had woken him.

Phil stretched out, shaking the grogginess from his limbs.

Then he touched his singed tail before roaring angrily at the dream cloud with a newfound strength. "I'm gonna grab that cloud and swing it around till there's no tomorrow!" he shouted out into the forest before turning to the sleeping Fortune, "And I'm gonna do it for you, my friend."

Words began to tumble passionately from Phil's mouth, as he felt the roar rise from deep within himself:

Hey you — cloud! Yeah you!
I dreamt you up but you got the best of me.
Hey you — cloud, you went too far!
You zapped the zest in me.
But you won't get the rest of me.
I'll get you, cloud — you're mine!
It just might take some time,
I'll get you yet, I'll make a bet,
I'll get you cloud, you're mine!

Won't let that cloud wreck my day,
No shadows will be cast,
Won't let that cloud darken my way,
I'll get you cloud at last!

Phil ran off into the forest after the cloud, leaving Fortune alone at the camp site.

As the last sparks of the fire crackled into nothingness, Fortune awoke. It was still gray and dreary in the devastated forest. Phil was gone. Feeling lonely, she fixed her hair and went to a nearby stream where she rinsed her face clean of yesterday's dirt. She heard some howling sounds in the distance.

Feeling frightened, Fortune picked up a stick and found a tree stump to hide behind. Her heart began to beat faster and faster as she felt more and more alone and afraid.

Then through the trees came a ray of sunlight...Fortune remembered a day in the Silent Land in the sky...

The clouds were sunny and rainbow colored. Fortune and the other Mimes held invisible sticks as they followed Monsieur Silence in a line, miming the act of walking a tight-rope. They held the stick horizontally in front of them for balance, careful only to take one step forward at a time. They took one step at a time... One step at a time....Keeping the balance.

Fortune snapped out of her daydream to find herself walking along the ray of sunlight like a tight rope holding the stick she had picked up for balance. She made her way delicately along the thin glowing ray and through the frightening gray forest. She saw Monsieur Silence in her mind's eye taking one step, then another... And she did too. She took one step at a time.

Eventually she came to a sunlit pathway where she discovered Phil's large footprints. As her concern grew for her friend, she followed the foot prints intently. To her relief, she soon found Phil. She ran towards him excitedly, waving and jumping for joy.

But Phil was standing at the edge of a cliff! A steep drop into a canyon far below lay before him. When Fortune finally reached him she stopped short and looked out in the same direction as Phil. The dream cloud was hovering just beyond the cliff.

"It must be out of reach for a reason, huh?" Phil pondered. "But I want that cloud and I'm gonna get that cloud." Fortune looked up at the cloud just as Phil began to roar again.

I'll get you cloud you're mine!
I'll get you cloud this time!

Suddenly, the cloud floated closer to them. Phil reached out for it, coming closer and closer until he finally managed to grab the cloud and pull it towards them.

"I got it!" he roared with joy as the cloud came upon them and completely covered him and Fortune. It was all fuzzy inside; they couldn't see a thing!

"There's nothing here... Hey, I can't see you!" Phil called out as Fortune tried to push the fuzzy white cloud out of her eyes so she could see. But everything remained a blur...

Chapter 11:

New City
"Be A Star Dance Studio"

Fortune and Phil were surprised and confused to suddenly find themselves peeking into a ballroom dance studio in New City with young dancers practicing their moves. Indeed, the children were rehearsing the Merengue in unison. Fortune and Phil stood peeking in wide-eyed awe.

"How did we get here?" Phil whispered to Fortune. She shrugged looking around with wonder and smiling. She had no idea.

"Look – they're dancing the Mambo now!" Phil continued, talking about the young ballroom dancers. "Wow! They're outrageous," Phil said starting to move his feet to the music. "I could be out there, right?" he asked Fortune. She smiled back, nodding her head enthusiastically, in agreement.

The young dancers suddenly caught sight of Phil - he wasn't small enough to hide — some pointed saying "a big puppy!" and then all of them ran over to pet him. Never having seen a lion before, they seemed to think he was no more than a big orange dog. Surrounding him, they laughed and petted Phil and hugged him — and he loved every moment of it.

"Oh look, a Mime too!" they said in unison as they saw Fortune crouched beside her lion friend. They laughed and giggled at the Mime. Fortune created the illusion of floating with an invisible balloon. Then they started to foxtrot around the big puppy — otherwise known as Phil the lion! They encouraged him to dance, so he got up and started to move with them through the studio, carefully and coordinated. The young ballroom dancers were delighted and they affectionately applauded his movements and petted him for his efforts.

"I am dancing like a pro. I'm leaping and spinning all over the place," Phil said to Fortune, with genuine delight. By now the children had started to dance and leap to a different beat, a louder one — hip hop! Phil was so happy he danced with the children from one end of the studio to the other. Fortune smiled and picked invisible flowers and threw them all over the studio like fantastical confetti.

As Phil danced, he was as happy as he had ever been. The music softened. Together, he and the children danced and laughed. He picked the children up and spun them and they held hands and twirled together. Now they all danced a beautiful waltz.

And then, in his joy, Phil's eyes starting tearing. He smiled and waltzed with big tears in his eyes. He tried to hide it but simply couldn't. It was too obvious, especially coming from such a big creature as Phil. Fortune looked at him with wide eyes and open arms, as if to say, "What's the matter?" Fortune and Phil stopped for a moment as the children continued joyfully waltzing around them.

Phil whispered to her, "Oh, wow, I miss the forest and the other animals. I left the forest in a shambles and I gotta go back and help. I don't know how I can help, but I know that's where I gotta go! I gotta get home to the forest and help the animals!" Fortune stopped for a moment. She looked at Phil and he knew she understood. Phil saw a tears appear in her eyes too.

And they both smiled.

Now with joy, Phil picked Fortune up over his head and started to spin. The young dancers circled them as Phil spun around and around with Fortune in his arms above his head. Around, around and around again! They waltzed and spun.

They were all together laughing and playing when the children's teacher came back to the studio. *She was shocked and horrified to find a huge lion in the dance studio!*

"Help! Help! The children are being attacked by a lion!" she screamed. Running to the wall, she immediately pulled the big red fire alarm, which started blaring a siren so loud the whole city could hear it.

Fortune held her ears in pain having never heard anything so loud. Phil stopped spinning and slid across the studio floor with Fortune on his back knocking into the children dancing around him who fell like bowling pins with legs and arms flailing. Trying to help the children, Phil grabbed them with his paws and they grabbed him back and all tumbled together in a big pile. More teachers ran in and screamed, "Help! The children are in danger! A raging lion! "

Two firemen ran in holding axes and nets and they pounced to catch Phil. Phil started running and spinning in circles trying to escape capture! The children started crying seeing that Phil was in danger. Just as a net was flying over his head, Fortune jumped under the net and was caught instead. Phil tried to help her escape the net by grabbing it with his teeth and ripping it open so Fortune could run. The firemen saw Phil bare his teeth and came after him with the axe.

"Save the children!" they yelled to each other. Phil ran the other way and out the back door. "A Mime?" said the firemen both at once. "Yes! Save the Mime too!"

"Children come here!" the teacher called out in distress as she attempted to gather them together. "Are you hurt? Oh dear! Get an ambulance!"

"We're ok!" they yelled and cried, confused by her panic.

Fortune saw Phil escaping out the back door and ran into the middle of the floor to block the firemen as they ran after him. Fortune began to throw invisible mime flowers all over the floor. The firemen slipped and tripped on the invisible flowers! Getting up confused and looking around, they could not see what they had tripped on. "Call for back up! The beast escaped!" one fireman yelled, while the other called. Soon, many fire trucks barreled down the streets of New City coming from many different fire stations.

The fire engines converged and created a traffic jam at the studio with sirens blaring. Firemen raced out in all directions trying to find a raging lion. "It's a huge raging and dangerous lion", yelled one fireman. "He went that way!" yelled the other. Firemen ran through the streets searching as more angry people bravely joined them. Soon, there were hundreds of people scouring the streets looking to capture the huge orange lion who they thought had harmed the children.

Among the sirens and confusion, the teachers stayed with the crying children who were asking, "Where's the puppy? What did the puppy do wrong?" One teacher was telling a reporter, "A huge orange lion with big teeth attacked the children in the studio as they danced. He tried to attack the Mime too. Look how he tore the net to shreds attacking the Mime!"

Helicopters started flying with loud announcements and radio and TV stations warned the city dwellers. All children and all the people closed their doors and windows. The streets were now empty except for the huge angry mob searching for Phil.

Phil was hiding in a dumpster and had tears flowing down his furry face. He didn't know why they were trying to catch him, but he knew they meant business. He had to escape to the deep forest. He peeked out of the dumpster, looking for Fortune. "Where is she?" he said out loud as the tears blurred his eyes. "What if they hurt her...." he said. "NO!" He crouched down and jumped out of the dumpster and roared the loudest and longest roar he had ever roared. The dumpster shook and the buildings shook while frightened people peeked out of their windows and trembled. He ran full speed right down the center of Main Street to go and save Fortune.

Fortune was safe over by the studio but stood in tears worrying about Phil. Some of the children were crowding around her saying, "Where is the puppy...What's wrong?" She hoped that Phil was far, far away by now.

But no! Lunging down the street came Phil with the mob

following right behind him. There were hundreds of people with nets and axes and sticks yelling, "Get him!"

Fortune began waving wildly at Phil, jumping up and down and pointing to him to go the other way to the forest. He turned to stop the oncoming mob, but it was too late. They threw a net over Phil and put chains on his paws. Having the lion trapped, the mob cheered and raised their hands celebrating their success in bringing the beast down.

The children cried. Fortune jumped up and down in front of the firemen and the mob trying to stop them.

"Someone quiet down this Mime," one of them said without thinking.

The mob dragged Phil towards a cage. As they dragged him over, Fortune ran over and made an invisible wall to block them from the cage. Colors flowed as Fortune created the wall. The mob was stuck and confused and started to kick the colorful transparent wall.....and then they started kicking Phil too.

Fortune distraught, tried to dissolve the wall so she could reach Phil. But the wall kept blocking her. She ran back and forth banging her fists against the invisible wall which was blocking her from her friend.

Finally, she stopped.

She opened her arms wide, took a wide stance and a deep breathe and mustering all her energy, she opened her mouth wide, and Fortune the Mime yelled out loud,

"STOP!"

The wall dissolved.

The colors dissipated.

The mob all froze in place.

...And then they all started to laugh.

"A talking mime!" they taunted walking right through the wall. Frantic, Fortune kept trying to make a wall reappear but to no avail. "Get this talking mime out of here," someone sneered.

Then, suddenly, in the midst of all this loud noisy taunting a rainbow appeared from high in the sky. It was a huge circular swirling rainbow! Simultaneously a cloud lowered down over everyone making a thick fog. The fog was full of sparkling rainbow colors and no one could see through it. It covered everyone and everything. Every move anyone made created a swirl of color. New City was a foggy sparkling and colorful mess!

Slowly the rainbow colored fog lifted, and the firemen and the mob, the children and the teachers, all saw an amazing sight—hundreds of mimes all sliding down the long rainbow from high in the sky! Each was holding a different colored umbrella on which they floated down from the clouds of Silent Land. Fortune jumped for joy and Phil said, "Wow!" Someone in the mob yelled, "Watch out! The Mimes look very mad!"

The Mimes circled around Phil and Fortune and the angry mob. They began making an invisible wall separating Phil and Fortune from the mob. The mob backed away and stood in awe watching the golden lines of force become a glowing wall. The invisible wall glowed a transparent gold. The Mimes then opened invisible doors in the wall and went through to the other side to help Phil out of the net and chains. Then they shut the doors behind them and disappeared.

The mob went up to the golden wall with hatchets and sticks but no one could get through it. They tried to push the wall but bounced right off of it. They tried to hit the wall but nothing would make a dent. The golden stream of light was too strong. The mob was dumbfounded. Each one stopped and stood still, seeing and feeling the golden glowing wall. One by one, they dropped their weapons.

Then there was silence. All became completely silent. The mob all looked up the wall fearing the worst. Flying over the golden wall there came.... flowers.... hundreds of flowers! Yes, hundreds of beautiful flowers came flying over the golden glowing transparent wall. More and more and more flowers! Hundreds, thousands of beautiful flowers! They appeared and disappeared and reappeared again. The sweet scents of roses and daffodils and all kinds of other flowers filled the air. The streets of the entire city became covered knee-deep in colorful flowers.

The children squealed with delight and played in the flowers. The firemen and mob softened as they breathed in the wonderful scent. Soon all the people were calm and smiled as they looked around at the beautiful flowers. Tears rolled down many faces. Many held hands. Everyone stopped to smell the flowers.

Then the flowers disappeared. The wall disappeared. All the Mimes disappeared. And Fortune and Phil disappeared too. Way up above in the sky was the rainbow. Floating up the rainbow were hundreds of Mimes holding different colored umbrellas. They floated up, up, up until they disappeared into the colorful clouds in the sky. And one other cloud – a dream cloud - floated away towards the forest with Fortune the Mime and Phil the Lion.

New City hasn't been the same since. The TV reported that the lion had been driven back into the forest and the city was safe. Many from the mob received Medals of Honor for saving the children from the raging orange lion with big teeth. The report claimed a fog had covered the city and that heavy rain was in the forecast. No mention was ever made of Mimes with umbrellas or of rainbows and flowers or of a transparent golden wall. Yet, the scent of flowers is still everywhere in New City.

Chapter 12:

Dreams Become Real

Phil was holding Fortune's hand in his paw as the cloud they were in lifted. Both of them looked around, failing to comprehend what had happened.

"We're back!" Phil was the first to speak. Well, Phil was always the first to speak! "I am so glad to be back!" Then he added softly as he looked up, "Was that a dream?" They both looked up to see the dream cloud float away and dissolve.

Fortune shrugged. She really didn't know.

"It must have been a dream," Phil said with his words laced with hope and anxiety. "I followed my dream and I learned to dance. Isn't that right? Isn't it, pal?" he persisted. Fortune had to agree. She nodded in agreement.

They looked around at the forest. Fortune found a small

egg and placed it in a nest that lay on the ground. Phil picked it up, leaped high up placing it back into its tree. The birds of the forest flapped their wings in the same manner a person would clap their hands, and began happily filling the forest with song.

The tree in question became filled with light and color before their eyes. Gracefully, Phil and Fortune continued to repair the damage Phil had done earlier. Phil leaped through the air and pushed a boulder out of the stream. The fish jumped, happily clapping their fins. Phil replaced the water lilies as he danced and glided down the river, jumping from rock to rock. The frogs jumped with glee.

Phil was on a roll. He swept the leaves from the forest floor and tossed the broken branches to the side. Fortune pointed to a mole's hold that had fallen in. Phil dug up the dirt and moles giggled with glee – they too had their home back! Soon the sounds and colors of the forest were back in full force and all was well. Fortune twirled happily and bowed to Phil, acknowledging his good work.

"I couldn't have done it without you! Friends like you are worth a fortune!"

Fortune put out her hand for him to shake, and Phil obliged with a big smile spreading across his furry friendly face. Fortune flew up and down through the air again with Phil's strong handshake.

"You showed me that my fortune is here," he said to her, pointing to his heart – "From now on I will call you Fortune the Mime." Fortune jumped for joy!

Later that day, Phil lay against the base of a willow tree.

"What's your dream, Fortune? You must have one, don't you?" he inquired. Fortune motioned to show him she is searching for her voice. She wants to be a singer!

"A singer..... Yeah! I could see that. You would make a great singer. I bet you can do it," he encouraged. Fortune stood for a moment in thought looking insecure. "You gotta follow your dream you know," he told her. "My best friend ever showed me that." Fortune, nodded, knowing in her heart that he was right. She looked off into the distance and smiled.–Phil encouraged her, "I know you can do it, Fortune! Ya gotta go for it you know."

Fortune stood still.

Phil ran up to her and gave her a big hug saying, "I know exactly what you are saying. And I hear ya loud and clear! I want you to stay here and dance with me but I think for now you gotta go sing. Yeah! Sing and sing real loud and throw invisible flowers and stuff like that .... That's what you gotta do!"

She smiled.

Phil continued encouraging her, "You do sing Fortune! To all the animals, to the people in the city and to me! I hear it already even though you don't make a sound! Now you just gotta believe it and do it."

Together they danced lightly together through the forest. Birds and moles and all the creatures peeked their heads out. Birds tweeted and moles burrowed and squirrels munched and all the animals scurried about. Fortune looked up to the clouds and in the far distance she saw the rainbow ....a circular rainbow and a colorful cloud. She knew she was safe and knew it was the best and right and only way for her to go—to follow her dream.

And Phil knew too. Somehow or other – yes he knew.

Fortune looked towards the big city. Somehow she felt drawn towards the people in the city.

Her invisible heart strings pulled gently that way....she turned and looked and knew she was on her way to great new expression and adventures.

"This ain't goodbye, Fortune. I'll be listening for your song! And you will sing and I will dance... yeah with those kids too!" He roared big and loud. "We're gonna be together again. We will ya know. I know it! "

With that, Fortune silently disappeared into the forest towards New City. Phil lay back down under the willow tree with a big smile and closed his eyes, both sad and happy at the same time.

Phil's loud snoring could be heard throughout the forest. The willow branches were floating up and down with each breath. Phil was sleeping a sound, sound sleep. But eventually a few birds flew by, managing to wake him up with their chirps and tweets.

"Will you please...I'm trying to..." he mumbled in response. But they got him up and pushed him out from under the tree. A big tuxedo with embroidering "World's Greatest Tango Dancer" was hanging there before him. Music started to sound from deep within the forest. Phil took the tuxedo down, put it on and started to dance without giving it a second thought. He was no longer afraid.

Smiling as he danced through the forest, he knew that Fortune the Mime was smiling too! He could feel that big smile and see her jumping up and down clapping. In the silence he could feel the music. To his joy and surprise he knew what she would be singing to him so loudly yet so softly, without words.

To himself he said out loud, "Silent Fortune I hear ya even though I'm not hearing nothin'!"

And as he listened to the silence, he thought he heard a female voice... his chest lifted and his hips swayed and he tangoed gallantly,

There is a place where you can go,
Where you can be what you want to be,
And do what you want to do,
Anytime, anywhere.

It's a place where you can laugh and dance and sing,
That's all you have to do.
I thought I couldn't be someone I'd like to be.
It took me a while to see the best inside of me!

Then, I saw that I could be,
Someone I'd love to be,
Dance like you'd like to dance!
Sing like you'd like to sing!

Plant a flower in the ground below!
Watch the flower grow and grow!
Be yourself and, yes, you'll see,
You can be what you want to be!

THE END
for now

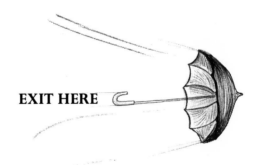

EXIT HERE

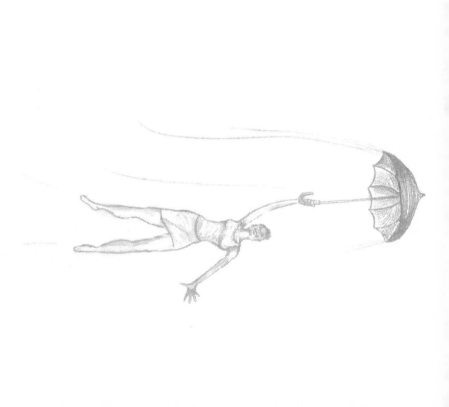

Acknowledgements

To everyone who helped a Mime write words:
I would like to thank, first of all, my parents, Tom and Gloria Carafa, for their love for life and support for me—even as they look on in bewilderment at my choices in life. Yes—you are my greatest inspirations!

I thank my beautiful niece Daniella Rosa and my dear friend Lynn O'Keefe Juliano for their great editing skills and support. Thank you to my sister Cynthia Rosa for offering wonderful ideas.

A special thank you goes to Andrew Whalley and Michael Susona for revisions on the book, to Joseph Dunham for your music renditions and to Ed Giordano for the beautiful illustrations. Also special thanks to Gregg Goldston for your great insight and support. Thanks to Joseph Dunham, Edith Baudoin and Dale Fuller for music, artwork and design.

To my real life Mime masters – Thank you Paul Curtis director of The American Mime Theatre for your brilliant mime procedures, creative process and forever friendship. Thank you to Marcel Marceau for our lunches together and hours of conversation and your uncompromising direction in my mime work. I miss you. You are both my real life inspirations for the character Monsieur Silence – the master Mime.

To My Yoga family – Bikram Choudhury thank you for teaching me to never let anyone take my peace. And thank you for showing me how to sweat puddles. To all my Bikram yoga students who I have had the great gift of leading thru our hot yoga series – thank you ! I love when you first go into Savasana after standing series and I get to see your hearts beating. What an amazing sight! This has been great inspiration for writing Silent Fortune.

To my Kauai Ohana –Lynn and Tom and everyone at Princeville Yoga - you have been such gems of inspiration for me. Big huge thanks to Makana David Martin, Psolar, Richard Kraft, Greta Kraft, Frederick Statile and Lotus White for your support in furthering my book and vision. And to all of my loving Ohana on the island of Kauai, who have taught me how to live from my heart, slow down and who have watched my mime performances and danced with me on the beach. To you all—the list is quite endless as is my gratefulness and love for you all!

And To my fellow performers, my clients, and my cohorts in NYC who have been a large part of my event production company –I thank you from the bottom of my heart for showing me how to be commercially viable and still creative and have a business in NYC that is led from the heart. Lee-Anne Gould, Bonnie Orshal, David Schulder, Rick Hostrup to name a few. Thank you.

A very special thanks to the book critics of South Seneca Middle School in Ms. Shaffers' 6th grade class, for their reviews and support prior to publishing.

There are so many people who have been my support team! If your name is not seen here – know that your name is on the top. It is in the silent space between the letters. I thank you … You know who you are! You are all my sweet angels of inspiration and I could not have completed this book without you.

And most importantly, I thank you – the reader!

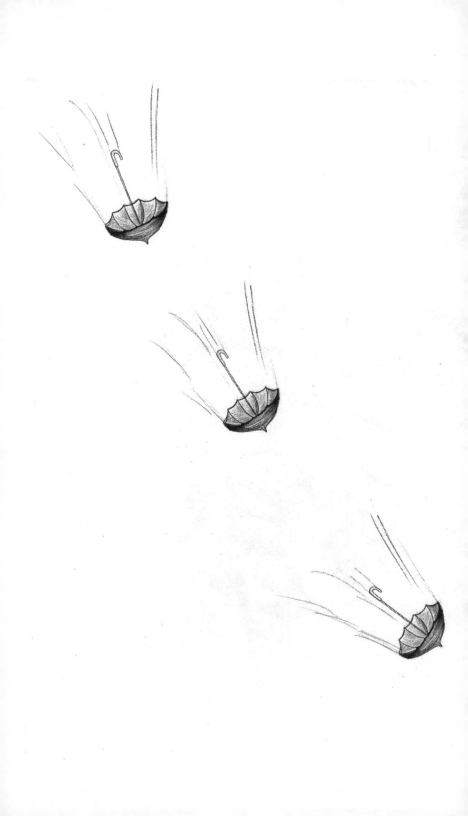

Footnotes

Information for this book can be found in:

- *your right brain*
- *the space between your thoughts*
- *lying on your back, arms out, watching clouds float*
- *the ocean wave just before it crashes*
- *the moment in-between your breathe*
- *rolling down a grassy hill and feeling everything swirl*
- *the times you laughed so hard that you fell to the ground*
- *feeling your heart beat and realizing it is beating on its own and wondering just how in the world that happens*

For More about the Art of Mime and for Mime Performance Demonstrations or Workshops by Janet Carafa:

www.artofmime.com
www.silentfortunethebook.com

And always remember:
Silence speaks louder than words.
(Source unknown)

CPSIA information can be obtained at www.ICGtesting.com
Printed in the USA
BVOW022327240412

288539BV00001B/12/P